Miami, Miami, Miami, Hurricanes

Drive, Drive, you Hurricanes

Keep right on goin, up that scorin'

Miami, Miami, Miami, Hurricanes

Drive on over the goal and on to victory.

M-I-A-M-I, M-I-A-M-I, fight, fight, fight.

Hello, Sebastian!

Naren Aryal

**Illustrated by
Amy Donohoe**

It was a beautiful fall day at the University of Miami. Sebastian the Ibis, the University's friendly mascot, woke up excited for the evening's football game.

Sebastian left his dorm room at the Stanford Residential College Commons and walked to the Hecht-Stanford Dining Hall where he had a delicious breakfast. Some students sat down at the mascot's table and said, "Hello, Sebastian!"

Sebastian's next stop was the Frost School of Music. The mascot ran into his favorite professor in the Rehearsal Center.

The professor was happy to see Sebastian. As they listened to the sounds of University of Miami students practicing, the professor waved, "Hello, Sebastian!"

From the Frost School of Music, Sebastian strolled over to the Miami School of Law.

As he approached the buildings, he ran into Miami alumni. The alumni remembered Sebastian from their days at Miami. They called, "Hello again, Sebastian!"

Sebastian then headed to Richter Library, where he ran into more Miami students. "Hello, Sebastian!" said the students.

The mascot checked out several of his favorite books. The librarian whispered, "Hello, Sebastian."

From the library, Sebastian strolled over to the Lowe Art Museum. After admiring the artwork, he ran into more University of Miami fans outside the museum.

They said, "Hello, Sebastian!"

Sebastian's next stop was the Fieldhouse, the home of the Miami basketball team. The basketball players were practicing hard for the upcoming season.

Sebastian impressed the team with his dribbling skills. The team shouted, "Hello, Sebastian!"

Finally, Sebastian arrived at Sun Life Stadium – home of the Miami Hurricanes.

Miami fans were excited for the football game and happy to see their favorite mascot. Fans cheered, "Hello, Sebastian!"

It was time for the Miami football team to take the field. They were led by their fearless mascot, Sebastian!

As the team emerged from the locker room, players cheered, "Hello, Sebastian! Go Hurricanes!"

Sebastian watched the game from the sidelines and cheered for the home team. The Hurricanes scored!

"Touchdown, Sebastian!" called the team's quarterback as he ran into the end zone.

At halftime, the Band of the Hour ran onto the field and performed the school's fight song. Everyone cheered,

"Let's Go 'Canes!"

Meanwhile, Sebastian decided to visit some students in the stands. Students called, "Hello, Sebastian!"

The football team played hard and beat its rival! The players and coaches celebrated the victory!

Sebastian gave players high-fives. Everyone cheered, "Great win, Sebastian!"

Miami fans were thrilled with the big win. As Sebastian left the stadium, fans cheered, "Way to go, Sebastian!"

After the game, Sebastian was tired. It was a long day at the University of Miami. The mascot walked home and crawled into bed.

Good night, Sebastian.

The End